To James —

Belly Button Boy

Peter Maloney Felicia Zekauskas

Dial Books for Young Readers ⚜ New York

To our own Belly Button Boy,
born July 28, 1999

Published by Dial Books for Young Readers
A division of Penguin Putnam Inc.
345 Hudson Street
New York, New York 10014
Copyright © 2000 by Peter Maloney and Felicia Zekauskas
All rights reserved
Designed by Kimi Weart
The text of this book is set in OptiSchow Light.
Printed in the U.S.A. on acid-free paper
1 3 5 7 9 10 8 6 4 2

Library of Congress Cataloging-in-Publication Data
Maloney, Peter, date.
Belly button boy/Peter Maloney and Felicia Zekauskas.
p.   cm.
Summary: Having neglected to bathe, Billy is surprised to find
that a bush is growing from his dirt-filled belly button.
ISBN 0-8037-2542-6
[1. Belly buttons—Fiction. 2. Cleanliness—Fiction. 3. Stories in rhyme.]
I. Zekauskas, Felicia. II. Title.
PZ8.3.M31947Be2000
[E]—dc21   99-047947

*For the pictures in this book, Peter and Felicia used pencils,
(lots of) erasers, and gouache.*

Billy loved digging, the deeper the better.
And some of that dirt got under his sweater.

At the beach Billy buried himself in the sand,
And even his sister would lend him a hand.

When people told Billy, "You're covered with dirt!"
Billy just answered, "Well, dirt doesn't hurt!"

So, soon Billy's navel was filled like a cup
With all kinds of things that boys will dig up.

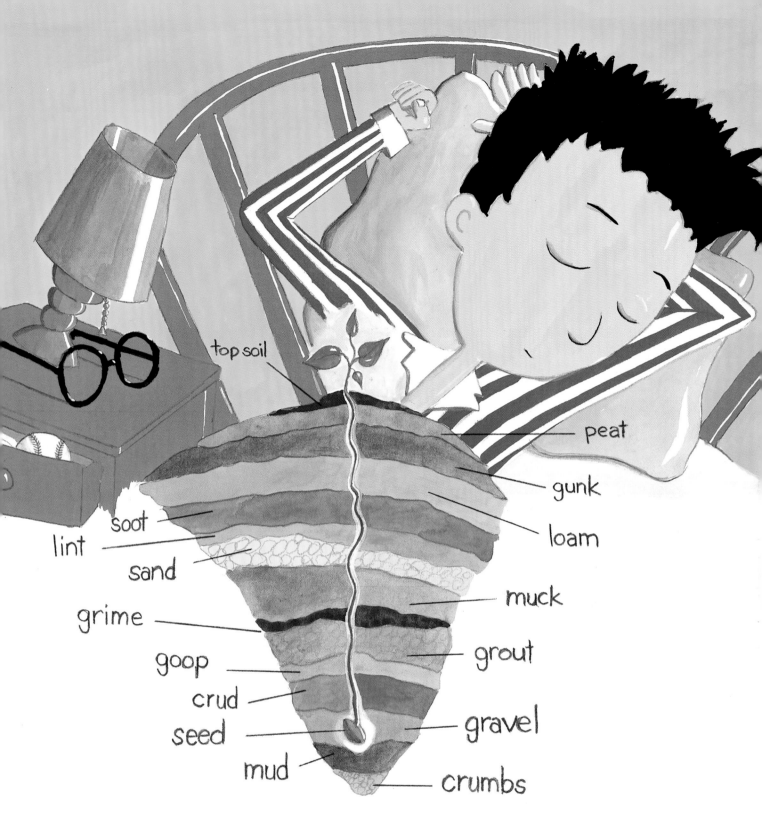

And under that dirt, that muck, grime, and grout—
The tiniest seed had started to sprout.

It grew through the night and then in the morning,
It woke Billy up without any warning.

There in his belly, a little bush stood,
And Billy just gasped, "This isn't good!"

This was something he just couldn't share—
He knew that his sister would tease him and stare.

And as for his friends, they'd mock him and jeer—
The things they would say, he'd rather not hear.

So, though it was warm, Billy put on long sleeves;
He had to wear clothes that would hide all his leaves.

He caught the school bus and kept to himself,
Then hid in the library behind a bookshelf.

He leafed through a book on what made things grow,
But the book didn't tell him what he needed to know.

Like how in the world had this happened to him—
To wake up one morning and have a new limb?

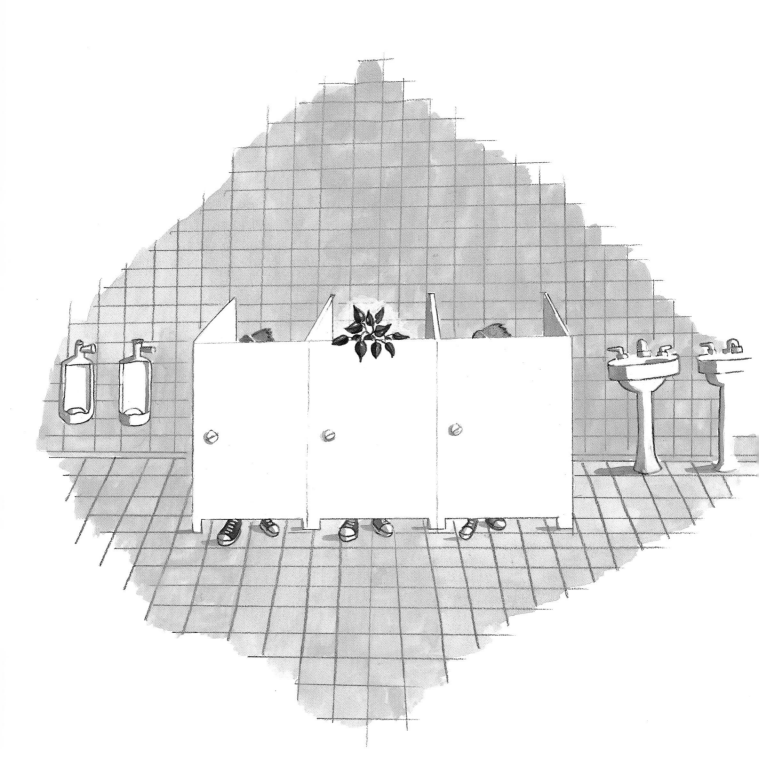

He went to the boys' room and, locked in a stall,
He saw that his plant was now several feet tall!

He raced past the gym and straight to the nurse.
He had to go home before things got worse.

The nurse sent him home, where up in his room,
He looked in the mirror and cried, "I'm in bloom!"

He knew it was time for him to reveal
The truth he had tried so hard to conceal.

His sister just screamed, "It's all that I need!
What can I say, 'My brother's a weed'?"
His father turned white, perfectly pallid.

He said to his son, "You look like a salad!"
Although the problem clearly had shocked her,
His mother just said, "Let's go see a doctor!"

Doc Dudley had seen him through fevers and flus,
But Billy's new problem was medical news.

"Your case is a matter beyond this physician.
I think a landscaper should treat your condition.

"Let's all go and hear what my gardener will say—
He sees things like this in his field every day."

The gardener was kind—wisdom shone from his eyes,
He looked Billy over and showed no surprise.

"The thing that you've got here, green, leafy, and fruited,
Could best be removed if it were quickly uprooted."

He gave a big tug, then uttered, "I've got it!
And now that I've got it, I think we should pot it!"

He looked down at Billy and said, "With your pardon,
A boy's belly button should not be a garden.

"You've got a great gift, son, for growing things green,
But your navel is one place you've got to keep clean."

Billy now washes himself head to toe,
Especially in places where dirt likes to go.

He doesn't want this to happen again,
Though the gardener did tell him:

"Dirt is our friend!"